THE WAY
A DOOR CLOSES

Hope Anita Smith

with illustrations by

Shane W. Evans

SQUARE
FISH

Henry Holt and Company
New York

For M. J. Auch
——H. A. S.

Thank you, God.
Dedicated to my uncle Booster
——S. W. E.

SQUARE
FISH

An Imprint of Macmillan

Library of Congress Cataloging-in-Publication Data
Smith, Hope Anita.
The way a door closes / Hope Anita Smith ; illustrated by Shane W. Evans.
1. Fathers and sons—Juvenile poetry. 2. Fatherless families—Juvenile Poetry.
3. Paternal deprivation—Juvenile poetry. 4. Children's poetry, American.
I. Evans, Shane W., ill. II. Title.
PS3619.M587 W39 2003   811'.6—dc21   2002067884

ISBN: 978-0-312-66169-4

Originally published in the United States by Henry Holt and Company
First Square Fish Edition: March 2011
Square Fish logo designed by Filomena Tuosto
www.squarefishbooks.com

10 9 8 7 6 5 4 3 2

LEXILE NP

The artist used alkyds on Strathmore paper to create the illustrations for this book.

Contents

THE WAY A DOOR CLOSES

Golden

There's a moment
right before morning that is
silent and still.
Grandmomma says it's a blessing
to experience.
I hug my pillow and try to
hold on to
this moment.
And then the day begins.
Daddy's razor roars.
The scent of Momma's cookin'
floats down the hall to me
till it tickles my nose.
I feel the vibration as my little brother
slap-bounce, slap-bounces
a ball to breakfast.
I open my eyes to see my sister
staring back at me,
secretly believing that she has
willed me awake,
and I hear Grandmomma's voice
singing a song of praise
for this new day.
My family is up,
just like the sun,
and we are all
golden.

Legacy

My brother and I
love to watch our daddy shave.
He sings as his razor
mows away his beard,
and we ask,
"When, Daddy?
When can we shave like you?"
And Daddy says,
"When you're older."
He rubs my brother's
smooth brown cheeks and says,
"You've got a ways to go, my man."
And my brother pouts
at the thought of how long
he has to wait.
And then Daddy turns to me
and says,
"C. J., on the other hand . . .
it's almost time.
You almos' a man."
I look in the mirror at my daddy's face
and try to imagine
the man I am going to be.

History Lessons

Grandmomma says she is a hard woman
because she has led a hard life.
So many obstacles blocking her way
when all she wanted to do was
be.
Signs made her drink from a
different fountain,
sit at the back of the bus.
Laws said she shouldn't go to
certain schools.
People said she couldn't learn.
They tried to move her around to
their way of thinking—
but now, she says, she knows the truth.
She says she is bent
but she is not broken.
She says if she isn't careful
she's gonna mess around and get her
second doctorate.
And then she smiles and loves me.
Hard.
She is a rock,
and I shall not be moved.

Interrogator Momma

On Sunday afternoons
it's just
the guys.
Daddy takes my brother and me
places that are
too rugged for women,
too grown-up for girls,
too adventurous for old people—
I mean, for Grandmomma.
My sister wants to come but
pouting and pleading
won't make it happen.
It's just
the guys,
and we've got to be on our way.
"On your way where?"
Momma asks,
trying to sound as if
she doesn't really want to know.

"Never you mind," Daddy says,
kissing her on the lips
and my teary-eyed sister
on the forehead.
Momma says,
"I know two little boys
who won't be going anywhere
if they don't give their momma
a hug and a kiss!"
And then Daddy is yelling,
"Run, men! Run like the wind!"
My brother and I
run out of the house.
We have no power against
Interrogator Momma.
 We have sold out
 for hugs and kisses before.

The Whole World in His Hands

I am looking at a photograph of
my family.
We are all smiling—
like someone has just told us
a good joke.
My momma sits stately
in a regal-looking chair.
My grandmomma stands
behind her because she's
"not that old."
My brother and sister are seated
at Momma's feet.
I am standing next to Grandmomma,
my hands laced together in front of me
in plain view,
because Grandmomma doesn't want
anyone to think that I am there
to hold her up.

And then there is my daddy.
He stands behind us
towering over us all.
One hand rests on my shoulder,
the other caresses my mother's.
Back straight and chest out,
my daddy is proud.

We are his world.

And he's got the whole world

in his hands.

Twice Blessed

In her heyday
my grandmomma was a knockout.
Daddy says, "She was so pretty
she stopped traffic.
She was a stone fox.
Truth be told, your grandmomma was
beautiful. Still is."

Grandmomma's eyes

light up.

She says, "Beauty is as beauty does,

and I did all right!"

We laugh and then Grandmomma

plops back down into now and says,

"That was a long time ago.

I had my chance at beautiful.

Everybody does.

But nothing lasts forever.

I got a little arthritis, varicose veins,

and strands of gray hair can vouch for that."

I look at my grandmomma's face and

grin from ear to ear.

I kiss her on the cheek and say,

"Well, then you lucked out,

'cause the way I see you,

that stuff

fixed it so you could be

beautiful

all over again."

Audition

Sunday mornings at our house
are full of music.
Grandmomma is singing.
She says she's auditioning
for the heavenly choir.
The music of her voice
gets us up and dressed,
gets us fed
and out the door.
Grandmomma is singing.
Her voice as rich as cream,
sure as tomorrow.
I close my eyes and try
not to let her see how her song
moves me.
Let her keep practicing.
She is music,
and I never want her song
to end.

Diamond in the Rough

Daddy has always spoken loud
of being black and being proud,
of honest pay for a job well done,
a father's dream for his oldest son.
He gives me words, each one a gem,
words I wish someone had given him.

Close Your Eyes

Scary movies don't scare me,
I only see what I want to see.
And when I get to the scary part
I don't hold my breath or stop my heart,
I close my eyes.

Grandmomma did the same
when telling of some wretched name
that she was called when she was ten,
a word she's heard again and again.
She closed her eyes.

Now Daddy's job has let him go,
and he doesn't want his pain to show,
but I can feel what he's not saying,
and I stand there—
silent, praying—
Daddy,
close your eyes.

Good White Things

Snow is falling
silently.
Little parachutes float
down to earth,
gently hitting the ground.
I tilt my head back
and make my face
a safe place to land.
And for a while,
I forget about
Daddy losing his job and
Momma working too hard
taking care of someone else's children
and not us.
Because this snow
makes me laugh as it
tickles down my neck.
And I smile because
Daddy was wrong.
There are
good white things.

The Dance

There is music coming from
the living room,
and I know that Momma and Daddy are
dancing their troubles away.
I tiptoe down the hall and peek
around the corner.
Daddy has one hand resting on the
small of Momma's back
while his other hand holds her
to his chest.
Momma looks up at him and smiles.
Daddy takes a step back, does some
fancy footwork,
and then he is dipping Momma
just like Fred Astaire dips Ginger Rogers
in those old black-and-white movies
Grandmomma loves to watch.
When Daddy brings Momma up,
he and Momma laugh and hug each other.
And then they are standing still
and Daddy's shoulders are shaking.
He is holding on to Momma
tight.
Momma cradles his head in her hands and
shushes him.

The music is still playing and they stand there,
Momma swaying back and forth
like a mother rocking her baby.

Job Hunt

Each day brings nothing.
But I just keep on praying—
God, give Dad a job.

The Way a Door Closes

When Grandmomma comes through a door
it closes quietly.
It is whispered shut
by the breath of God—
who acts as a doorman for
one of His good and faithful servants.
When my brother and I
go out the door,
it closes like a clap of thunder.
We are always in a hurry
to be somewhere.
My little sister closes the door
just so.
As if there were a prize for
getting it right.
My momma likes doors open.
It's her way of inviting the world in.
But last night
Daddy said,
"I'm going out,"
and he stood buttoning his coat
just so.
As if there were a prize for
getting it right.
Then he looked at each of us
a moment too long.

And when he went out the door
he held on to the knob.
The door closed with a
click.
I felt all the air leave the room
and we were vacuum-sealed inside.
I shook it off.
I told myself it was nothing
but
somewhere deep inside
I knew better.
I can tell a lot by
the way a door closes.

Geography Lesson

Lately,

my sister has become

obsessed

with a story about a kid

whose house and life

get all messed up

because of a tornado.

It's her favorite

and she's got a pair of ruby slippers

to prove it.

So, every night I read

about witches (good and wicked),

flying monkeys, and

a wizard

until she falls asleep.

It takes a while

but finally

we get to the end

and the kid in the book wakes up and

realizes

it was all a dream.

And I realize

my sister is crying,

and I can't figure out why.

She looks at me

through her tears and says,

"We aren't in Kansas anymore."

Not Today

As soon as I walk through
the door
I know that Daddy is still
gone.
I kiss Momma on the cheek
and taste the salt from her tears.
I swallow the lump in my throat
over and over again.
She looks me in the eye,
and I see
an invitation.
She is inviting me to join her
for a good cry.
But instead
I put my arm around her and
I tell her not to worry.
I will take care of her.
I will take care of all of us.
I say I can get a job after school.
I say I could even take a break
from school
until we get things squared away.
I say I'm not a little kid anymore,
she can depend on me.
And then Momma is wailing,
"Noooooooo!"
And she grabs me and

slaps me hard across the face
and the sting brings tears
instantly.
Momma looks relieved.
I hold my cheek and I say,
"Why, Momma? Why?"
And she hugs me hard
and through our tears
I hear her say,
"Time enough for you to be a man
tomorrow
but not today."

And One to Grow On

Today
I turned 13.
And there are 14 holes in my cake
where the candles used to be.
One for each year
and one to grow on.
Momma wants to know
what happened to them
and I tell her
I did it.
I took them out and threw them away.
One for each year
and one to grow on.
I don't need candles on my cake.
I don't want to close my eyes
and make a wish.
I'm 13 now
and I know how much it hurts
when wishes don't come true.

The Pull of the Moon

Once a month
the moon is full.
Grandmomma says
there's an invisible thread
connecting each of us to it.
She says sometimes she can almost
feel the moon
pulling on that thread.
She says sometimes it's so strong
folks can't help but
put on their traveling shoes.
I wonder if that's what made Daddy leave.
If he felt the pull of the moon.
Grandmomma says
once in a while
we get another full moon
in the same month.
A blue moon.
A second chance.
"Moons," Grandmomma says,
"are one of God's little gifts
to help us find our way home."

Photo Op

Every photo album we own
is open and sprawled all over my bed.
"What are you looking for?"
my sister asks.
"I can help you find it."
She's looked through these albums
a thousand times.
And although
she's not in every picture,
she knows that every picture is
of someone
who is connected to her.
I let her stay but I know she can't
help because I'm not looking for a person.
I am looking at pictures of Daddy.
I stare into each picture hard,
trying to read the face of my father,
trying to see if there is a sign saying
one day he will leave us.

Little Man

My brother is pounding on the door.

Rap, rap, rap.

"Let. Me. In."

Both sounds working together in

two-part harmony.

I am trying not to hear him.

I lie on my bed

with my fingers laced behind my head

and I smile big.

Because it feels good to be alone.

And even though I can't hear the silence,

when I close my eyes I can almost see it.

But then I hear the volcano

that is my momma's voice

erupt

as she calls my name,

"Cameron James!"

And I know that my solitude is over.

I open the door quickly.

Momma's eyes ask me if I've lost my mind.

My brother's face is tear-stained

and shows he has been betrayed by his hero.

Grandmomma pretends to take no notice

of the situation.

No one says a word.

This is not the silence I had in mind.

So I say,

"Sometimes

a man needs a little privacy!"

Grandmomma clears her throat and says,

"I reckon that's true.

Sometimes a man does need a little privacy."

She can't hold back a laugh when she adds,

"Now, you let your brother back in that room

'cause, I know for a fact,

we could fit the whole

tabernacle choir in there

and you'd still have enough privacy

for the amount of man you are!"

The Power of One

My grandmomma's hands hold
my hands and me
but mostly
they hold
everything together.

Going, Going, Gone

Momma is crying again.

In the background I hear Grandmomma

singing a hymn

and it becomes my plea:

O Mary, don't you weep.

Suddenly, I want answers

to questions I have been too scared

to ask.

I follow the sound of Grandmomma's voice

and find her rocking.

Eyes closed but turned toward heaven.

"Grandmomma,

Daddy's not coming back, is he?"

She stops her song but she keeps on

   rocking.

I'm afraid of her answer, so

I keep talking.

"We're supposed to be a family.

He should've stayed.

Now all my friends are going to know

that Daddy left us.

Just like Preacher's dad left him.

Just like Neecy's dad left her.

Just like them,

my dad left

me."

Grandmomma smiles and says,

"There are a lot of ways of leaving.

Your daddy

left

a while ago.

Now, he's just gone."

Grandmomma's China Bowl

Grandmomma's china bowl
sits
with its hands cupped
but open.
Always begging for more.
More mints.
More nuts.
More
of whatever is being offered.
And with each offering
it extends an invitation to
hands.
Never fearing
"empty" or
"gone."

Telling Tales

The teacher said,
"Just for fun,
everyone make up a story
using your wildest imagination."
I chewed on my eraser
for a long time before I
started to write
about a boy
just my age,
who wore pants that
covered his ankles
and shoes that didn't
hurt his feet.
He lived in a
three-bedroom apartment
with his mom and dad.
And the heat worked.
And the water ran clear.
And when he heard
loud popping sounds at night
he knew that it must be
the Fourth of July.
Oh, yeah,
and he lived happily
ever after.

Tell Me Something I Don't Know

I am sitting

across from my guidance counselor,

and I can hear what he's saying, but

I'm not listening.

"Your teachers tell me

you're not quite yourself.

I understand there's a problem at home.

These things happen.

You'll feel better if you talk about it."

I am trying to figure out why

I'm here.

My grades haven't dropped.

I haven't cut any classes.

This is a courtesy call.

Guidance counselor damage control.

I don't need this.

I am almost out the door

when I feel two hands drop anchor

on my shoulders.

My guidance counselor,

locking in on my eyes

for emphasis,

says,

"It's important that you understand

this is not your fault."

I shrug my shoulders free and wait a beat

before leaving.

I think to myself,

"Not my fault!

I know that.

I'm just having a bad day.

I'm not stupid!"

Dream

Daddy is leaving.
My momma falls to her knees,
clings to him,
crying hysterically,
"Don't go! Don't leave me!"
And then,
we
each in our turn
grab on.
Me to my mother,
my brother to me,
our sister to him.
A human chain.
The door opens,
and then Daddy is
outside.
He is lifted into the air.
We hang on.
Suddenly
Daddy is flying,
just like a kite,
and we are the tail.
Our holding on
is the thing that lets him soar.

When a Daddy Goes

Sister cries while she is sleeping

It's as if her eyes were leaking

Seems that our whole house is weeping

When a daddy goes

Brother's acting like a stranger

Eyes and words are full of anger

Warning signs, they all spell danger

When a daddy goes

Momma's hands are always praying

Listening for what God's saying

Holding tight for fear of straying

When a daddy goes

Grandmomma's voice is raised in singing

To God's promises she's clinging

All the joys that He is bringing

When a daddy goes

Me? I stare up at the ceiling

Think on all the things I'm feeling

Seems as if my head is reeling

When a daddy goes

It's not so much about his leaving

It's that he left a family grieving

Oh, what a tangled web he's weaving

When a daddy goes

Family Fire

The secret of my father's
leaving
spreads like wildfire
burning out of control before I can
escape.
My friends are keeping their distance.
They can't help me.
They can only hope
the fire is self-contained.
They can only pray
I'm not too badly burned.
I try not to add fuel to the fire,
keep all flammable words and feelings
to myself.
Everyone's eyes are on me.
There's something about
watching a fire.
Now I am the poster child
for families with problems.
Fathers, everywhere, will see my face
plastered onto signs,
and my slogan is
"Family fires,
only you can prevent them."

Schoolyard Sermon

My best friend, Preacher,
is being just that.
His sermon today is on fathers,
and I am his congregation.
"Dads are light.
They have no roots.
One strong wind, and they're
gone.
Out of here.
History.
And just like yesterday,
they don't come back."
I am quiet.
"You don't have to say amen,"
Preacher says.
"It's the truth anyhow."
I listen, but I can't say amen.
Preacher is wrong.
"My dad is coming back,"
I announce.
Preacher shoos my words away
with a wave of his hand.
"Man," he says, "that only happens
once in a blue moon."

I smile as I head to my next class
and I say,
more to myself than to Preacher,
"But it happens."

Winter Words

It is cold outside
but I am hot.
I am so hot I could melt
snow.
Momma is going
"out"
again.
"Out where?" I ask,
trying to sound as if
I don't really want to know.
"Never you mind," she says with a smile
as she kisses me.
And then she steps back and does
a twirl.
She moves like music.
And even though I am proud
to have the most beautiful momma
in the world,
I don't let it show.
"How do I look?" she asks me,
and I almost think about what
I am going to say.
Almost.
But then the words are
flying
from my mouth to my momma's ear.
"How should I know?"

I roll my eyes and the rest of me follows.

"Mind your manners," Grandmomma warns,

but it's too late for that.

My words are charging into battle.

"You and Daddy are still married.

And even if *you* don't,

we still miss him!

We still love him!"

Momma wraps her arms around me,

but I am as hard as a rock.

She talks softly.

"I know that, honey.

I miss him, too.

I just wanted my son to tell his ol' momma

how she looked."

I pull away and look her

dead in the eye

and say,

"You look like you forgot."

History Repeating (Almost)

Momma is trying to talk to me,
but there are so many words
swimming around in my brain
that I'm sure they will start to
leak out all over the floor if I let
any more come in.
So I walk out of the room.
I walk out the front door,
and I keep walking.
I am walking away from
all the things that are making me hurt.
All the things that are making me mad.
I am walking away
just like Daddy did.
I am leaving all my problems
behind
just like Daddy—
I stop.
Because
suddenly
I am seeing Momma's face
when Daddy left.
I turn back toward home
and I run.
I run so fast it hurts to breathe,
but I can't stop.

I don't stop until my arms are
wrapped around Momma's middle
and my "I'm sorrys" are lost in her lap.
My tears stain her sun-gold dress like
a sudden rain.
She lifts my head,
cups my face in her hands, and says,
"You just changed the course of history."
"How'd I do that, Momma?" I ask.
"You came back."

Temp Job

There was a time when
the stars had to be aligned
just so
to get me to be
"the best big brother in the world."
The one who took you with him.
The one who wanted to hang out with you.
But now
my brother has mastered the art of
getting to me.
He learned from our sister
(who, by the way, can get me to do
anything).
So, when he begs for a game of hoop,
even though I need to study,
I grab the ball and head for the driveway.
We run up and down
our cement court,
dribble, dribble, stop.
Dribble, dribble, shoot.
"Whoosh"—
my brother's word and
the ball going into the net
at the same time.

We play hard.

And I let him win.

Just like Daddy used to let me win.

I give him a high five and put him

in a head lock as we go inside.

"You done good," I say.

My brother looks at me and smiles.

"You sound just like Daddy."

For a minute I forget to breathe.

And then I smile because

I feel good carrying on the tradition

in my father's absence,

and I say, "Thanks, little brother,

but I'm just filling in."

Forgetfulness

It didn't seem right,
being happy while Daddy was
gone.
He wasn't dead
but still, I was in mourning.
Yesterday,
I forgot that I had
nothing to be happy about.
I forgot to remember
that this is a bad time,
a "no dad" time,
a sad, sad time.
I don't even remember
what was so funny, but
I do remember
I felt like I'd betrayed something—
the memory of my father—
because I laughed.
I laughed so hard
I cried.

Prodigal Son

Even before my brother and sister

yell out his name,

the muscles in my mother's hands

stop working,

and the plate she is drying

goes crashing to the floor.

My back is to the door,

but I can't turn around.

I am afraid this is a bad joke

and the laugh will be on me.

Grandmomma is not surprised.

She knew

what we all secretly hoped for.

No one actually heard the door

open

but we all heard it close.

And I breathe a sigh of relief

because

I know Daddy is home to stay.

Trust me,

I can tell a lot by the way a door closes.

Astronomy 101

All I can think about is
finding Preacher.
When our paths finally cross,
my chest is puffed out as I begin
the lesson.
"Preacher,"
I say,
"you know what a crescent moon looks like.
You know what a quarter moon looks like.
You probably even know what a
waxing gibbous moon looks like.
But let me tell you what a
blue moon
looks like.
It's my dad
coming home
after being gone for what seemed like forever.
He can't find enough words
to say how sorry he is.
But he keeps on.
Each word rooting him to us
like a tree
that's planted by the water and
he shall not be moved."